IF I WERE A TREE

IF I WERE A TREE

A TREE

ANDREA ZIMMERMAN

ILLUSTRATED BY

JING JING TSONG

LEE & LOW BOOKS INC.
NEW YORK

To Rachel — A. Z.

For my parents, T. T. and M. F. Tsong,
who introduced me to wild places — J. J. T.

If I were a tree, I know how I'd be.

My trunk strong and wide, my limbs side to side.

I'd stand towering tall, high above all,

My leaves growing big, and buds on each twig.

If I were a tree, that's how I'd be.

If I were a tree, I know what I'd feel.

The warmth of the sun, and squirrels on the run.

I'd feel nests on my bark, bats hiding till dark,

The climbing of boots, and worms by my roots.

If I were a tree, that's what I'd feel.

If I were a tree, I know what I'd taste.

The layers of land, the soil and sand.

I'd taste old buried bones, and pebbles and stones,

And waters that flood, and minerals in mud.

If I were a tree, that's what I'd taste.

If I were a tree, I know what I'd smell.

Sweet honey and bees, and skunk on the breeze.

I'd smell smoke in the air, the breath of a bear,

Old fungus decay, and rain on the way.

If I were a tree, that's what I'd smell.

If I were a tree, I know what I'd hear.

Far thunder's low growl, the hoot of an owl.

I'd hear snakes in a hole, the sneeze of a mole,

A rocky stream flow, the swishing wind blow.

If I were a tree, that's what I'd hear.

If I were a tree, I know what I'd see.

Hills misty with fog, the life in a log.

I'd see blossoms appear, and tiny new deer,

A web draped with dew, the dawn turning blue.

If I were a tree, that's what I'd see.

If I were a tree, I know what I'd love.

The wind's playful tugs, the humming of bugs.

I'd love smelling the pine, and geese in a line,

The taste of the earth, and every seed's birth.

If I were a tree, that's what I'd love.

If I were a tree, I know what I'd know.

That days come and go, and green leaves will grow.

I'd know branches can bend, and cold spells will end,

That spring will renew, and life carries through.

If I were a tree, that's what I'd know.

EXPLORING TREES

There are more than a trillion trees on Earth! You can use your five senses to get to know the ones that live near you.

SEEING

Look at the overall shape of each tree. Is it tall and lanky? Or short and bushy? Look at the leaves. Are they broad or needle-like?

TOUCHING

What does the bark feel like? Is it rough? Or smooth? Do the leaves feel fuzzy? Or prickly? Are there roots or seeds you can touch?

SMELLING

Some trees have fragrant flowers or zesty sap that you can smell. If you hug a tree, how does the bark smell? If you wrinkle a leaf, what scent does it have?

TASTING

You probably can't taste any of the trees that live in your neighborhood. But there are many trees that we do taste. We eat delicious fruits and nuts and spices from trees. Even chocolate comes from trees!

HEARING

On blustery days, you can hear the wind whistling through the leaves of a tree. You may also hear the birds and bugs that make their homes in the branches of trees.

There are more than 60,000 different kinds of trees on Earth!

You can learn more about the trees in your area using books like *The Tree Book for Kids and Their Grown-Ups* by Gina Ingoglia or a field guide for your state.

LEE & LOW BOOKS Inc., 95 Madison Avenue, New York, NY 10016
leeandlow.com

Edited by Cheryl Klein
Book design by Christine Kettner
Book production by The Kids at Our House
The text is set in Egyptian Bodoni Bold, with the display type in Folk.
The illustrations were created using traditional printmaking techniques,
which were then digitally collaged in Adobe Photoshop and Illustrator.
Manufactured in China by RR Donnelley
10 9 8 7 6 5 4 3 2 1
First Edition

Library of Congress Cataloging-in-Publication Data
Names: Zimmerman, Andrea Griffing, author. | Tsong, Jing Jing, illustrator.
Title: If I were a tree / Andrea Zimmerman ; illustrated by Jing Jing Tsong.
Description: First edition. | New York : Lee & Low Books, Inc., [2020] |
   Audience: Ages 4-8. | Audience: Grades K-1. | Summary: Two siblings
   imagine life as a tree, and envision what they would hear, feel, and see.
Identifiers: LCCN 2020042440 | ISBN 9781620148013 (hardcover) |
   ISBN 9781620149867 (epub)
Subjects: CYAC: Stories in rhyme. | Imagination--Fiction. | Trees--Fiction.
   | Brothers and sisters--Fiction.
Classification: LCC PZ8.3.Z495 If 2020 | DDC [E]--dc23
LC record available at https://lccn.loc.gov/2020042440